Fucks and Flowers

Adult Coloring Book

chelsea lea

This Book Belongs To:

_____

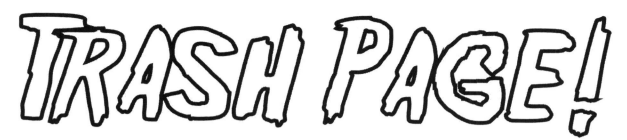

TRASH PAGE!

Use this page to test colors before you start coloring

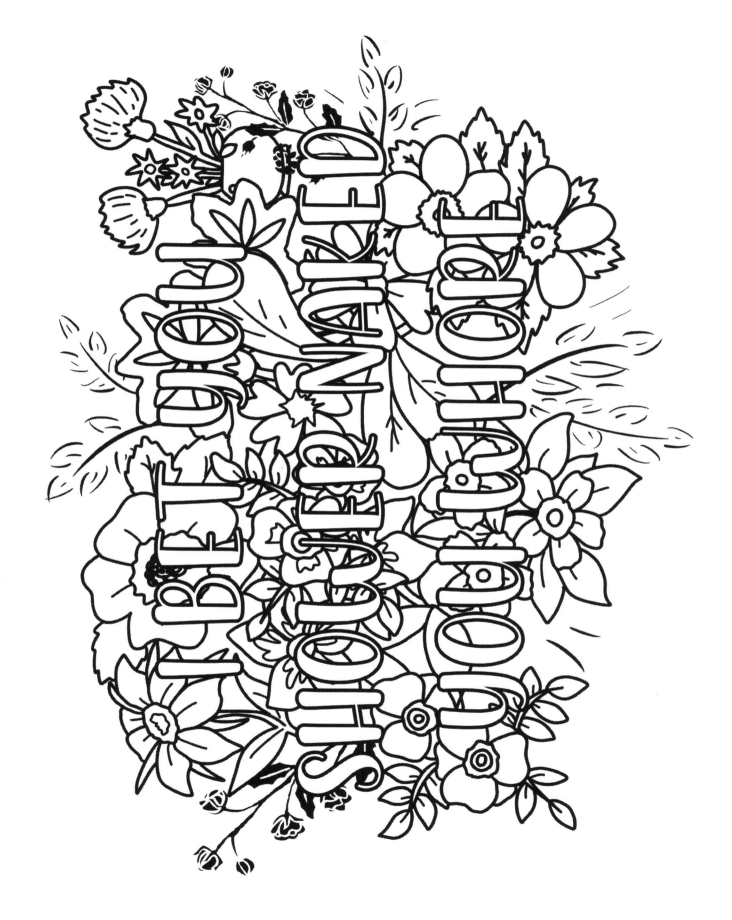

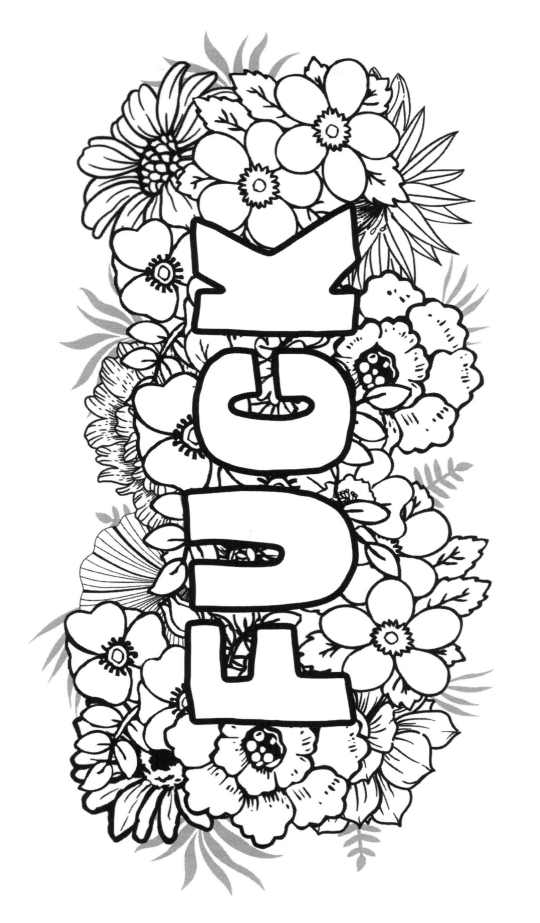

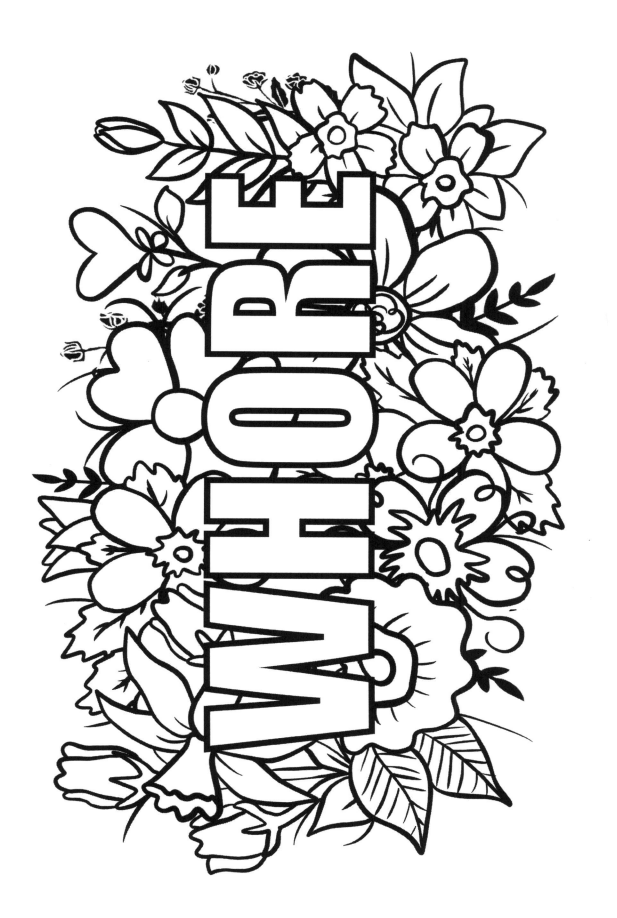

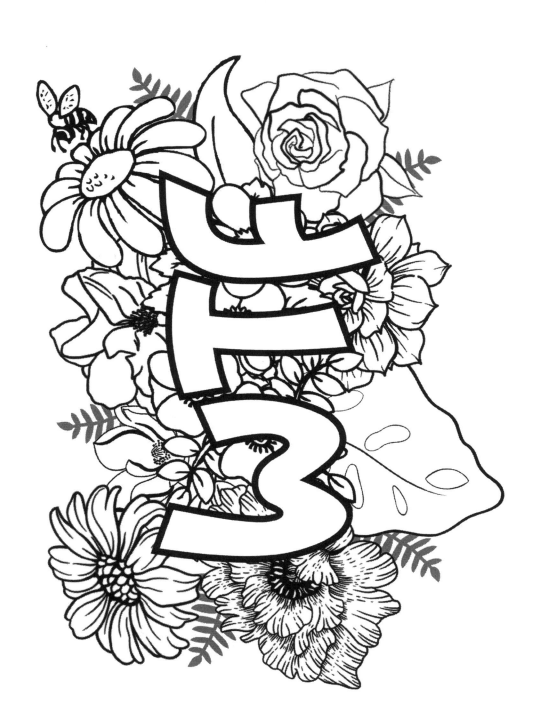

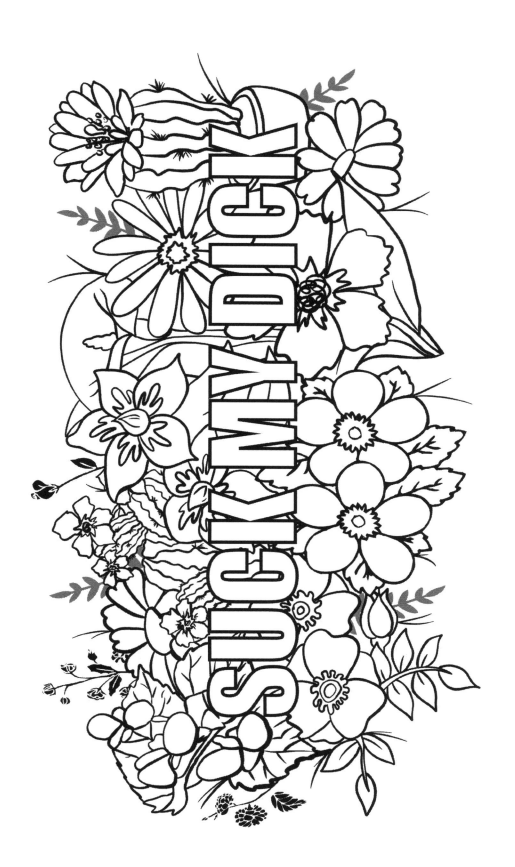

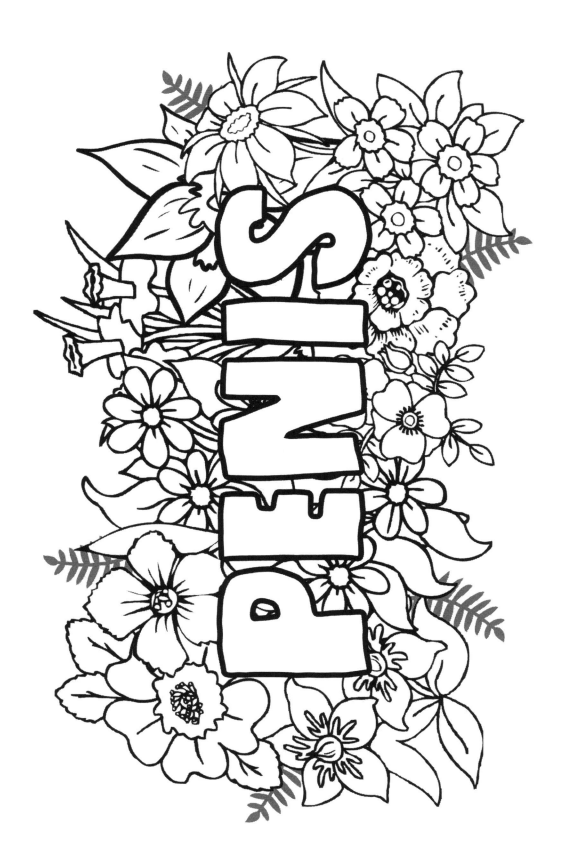

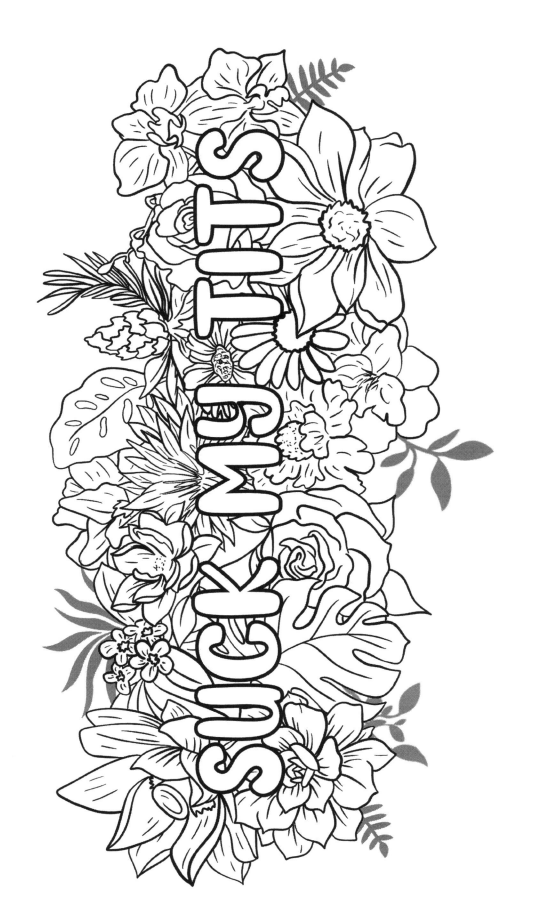

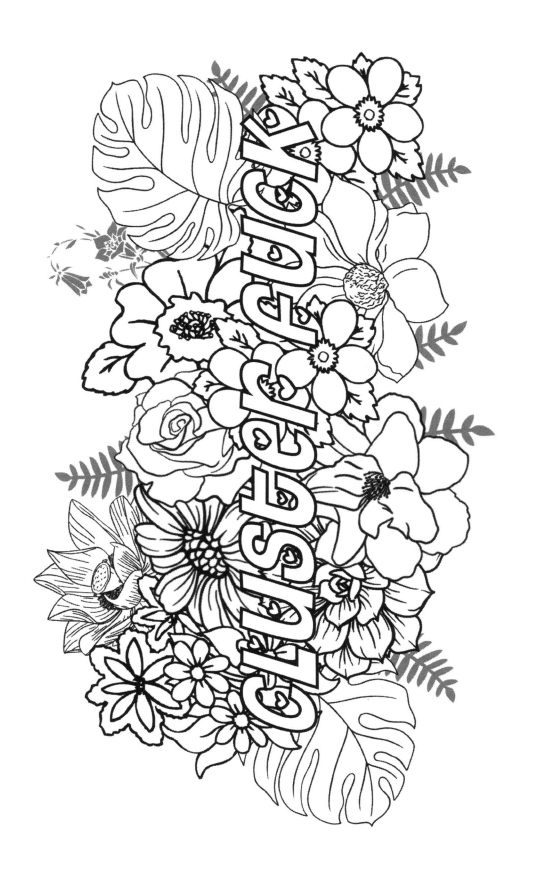

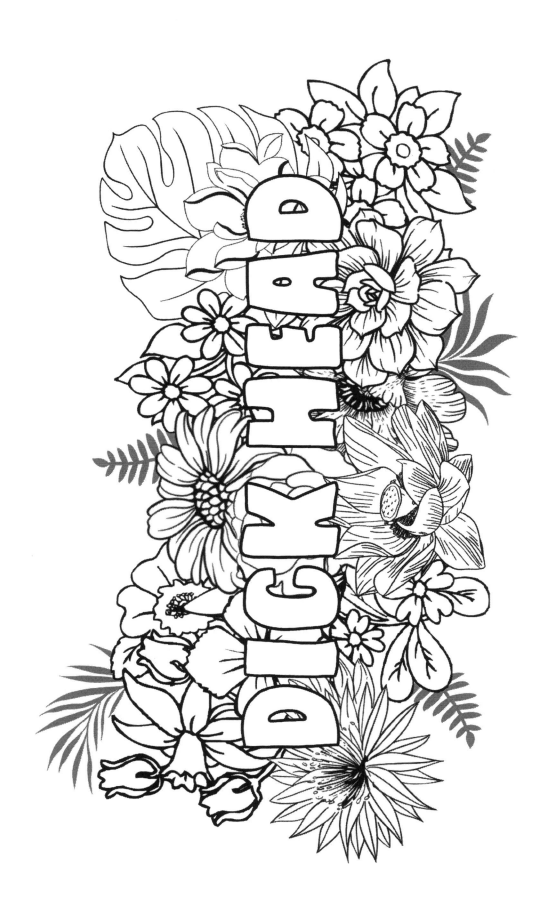

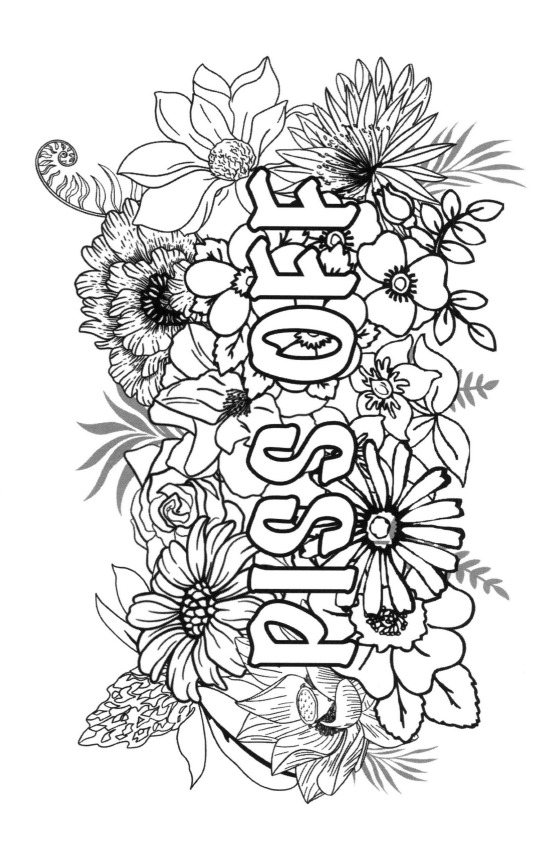

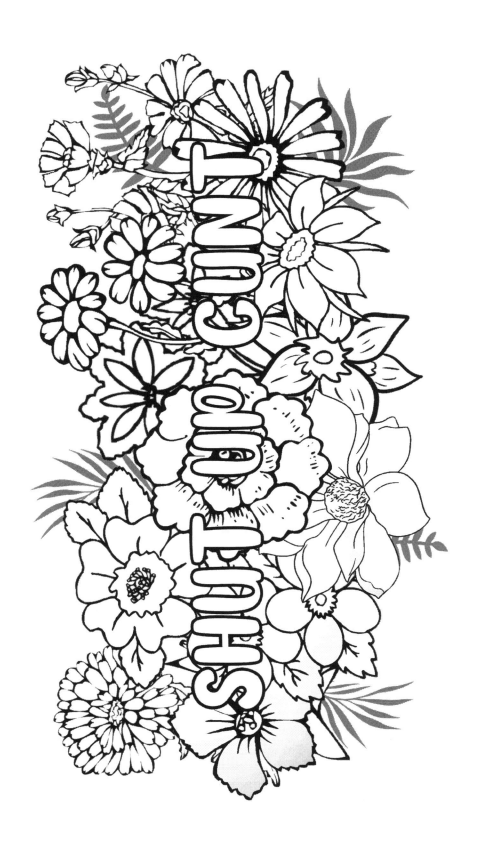

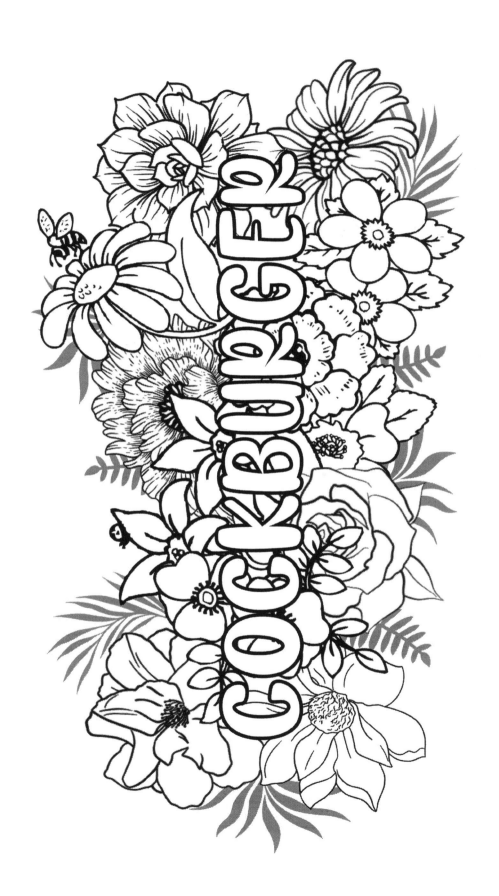

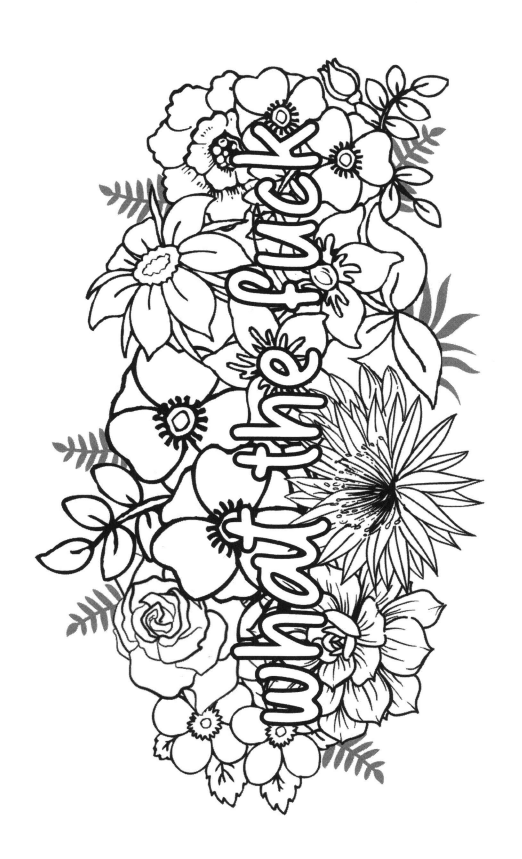

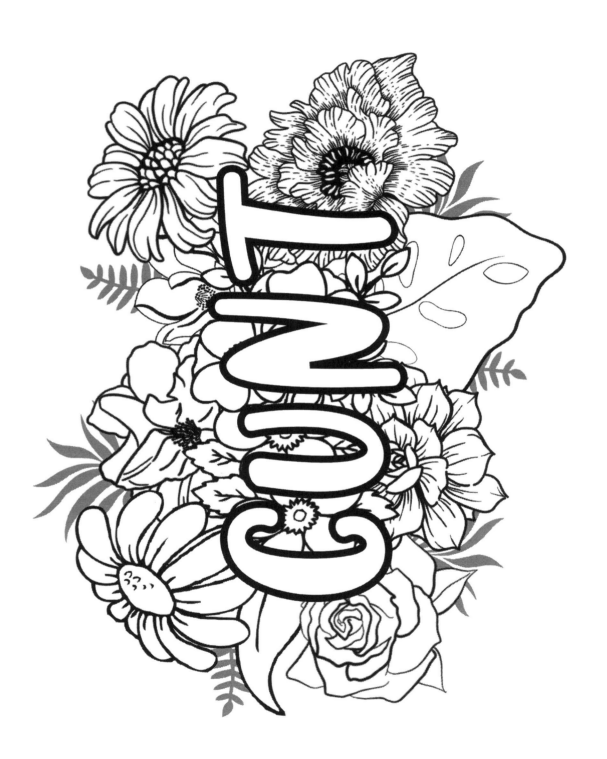

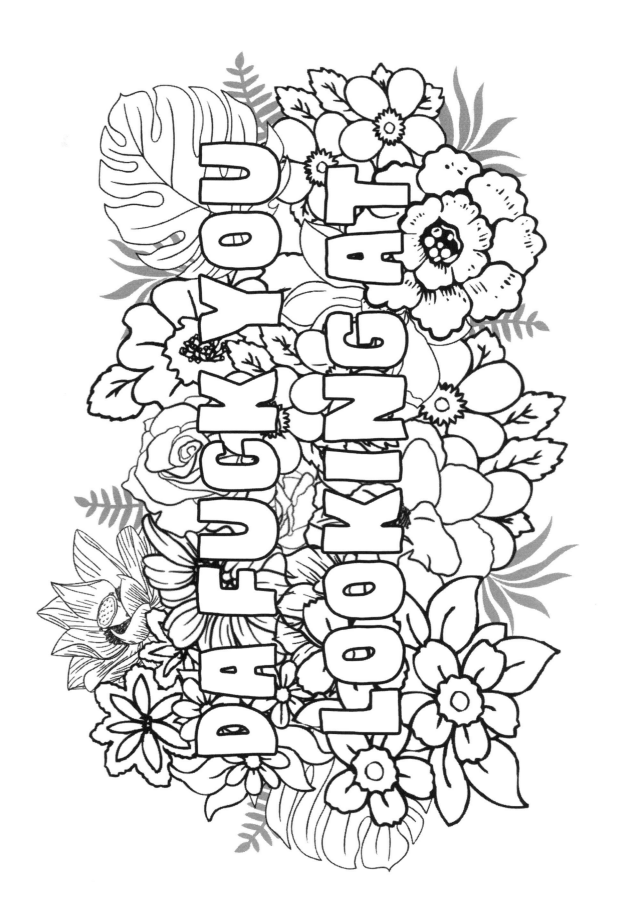

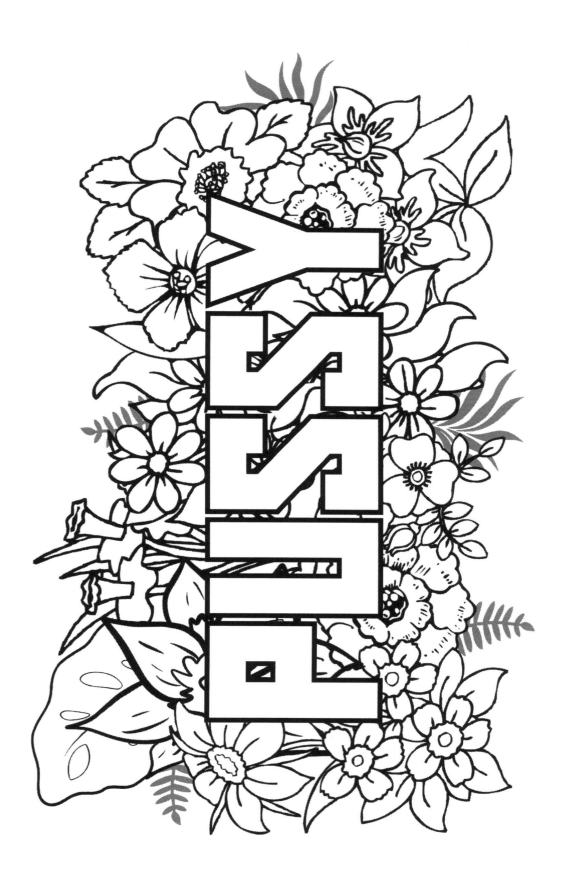

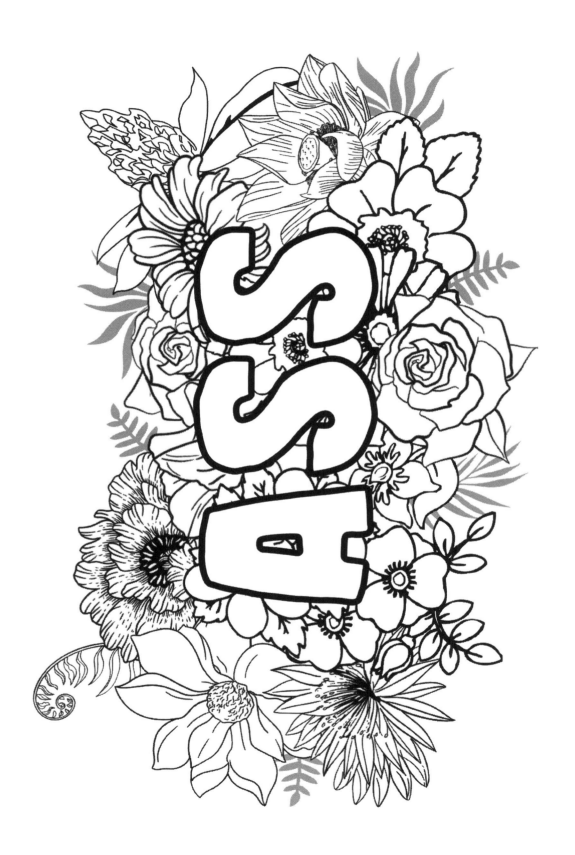

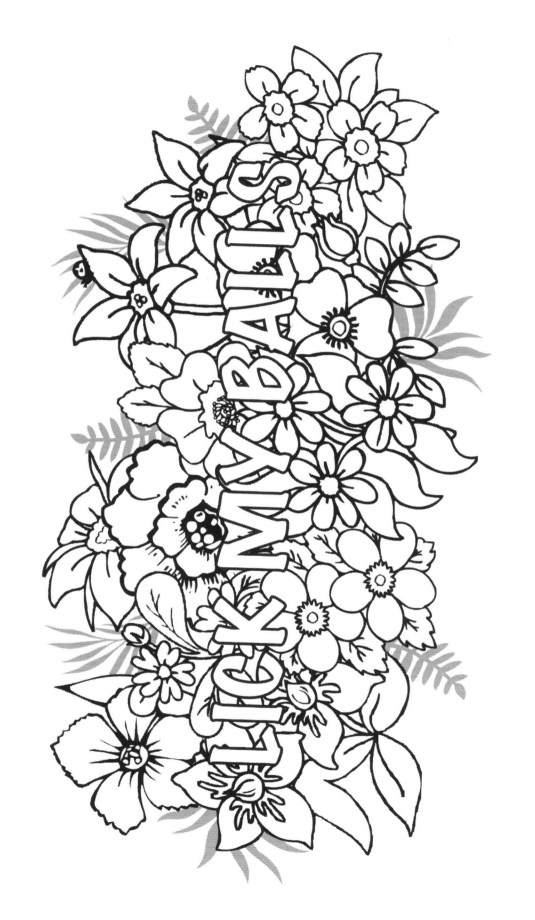

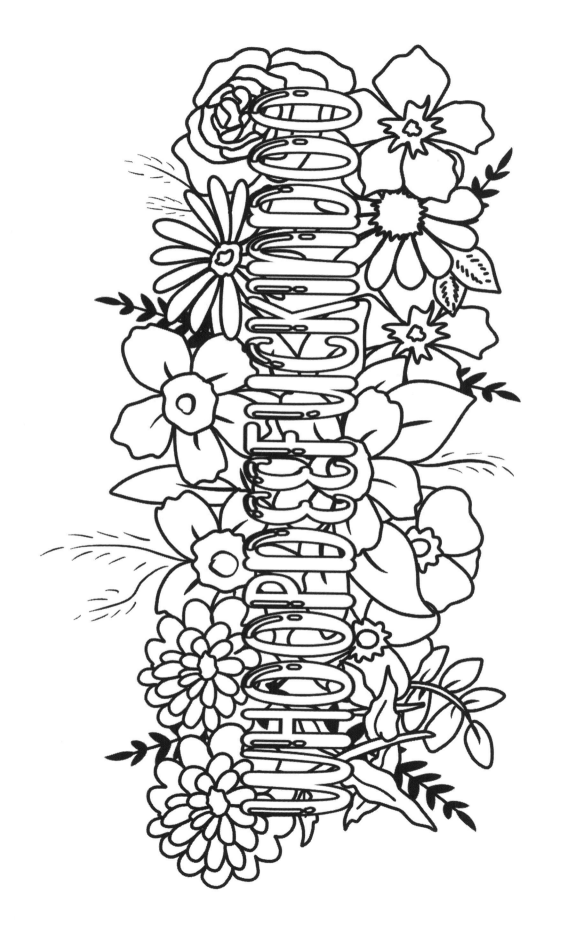

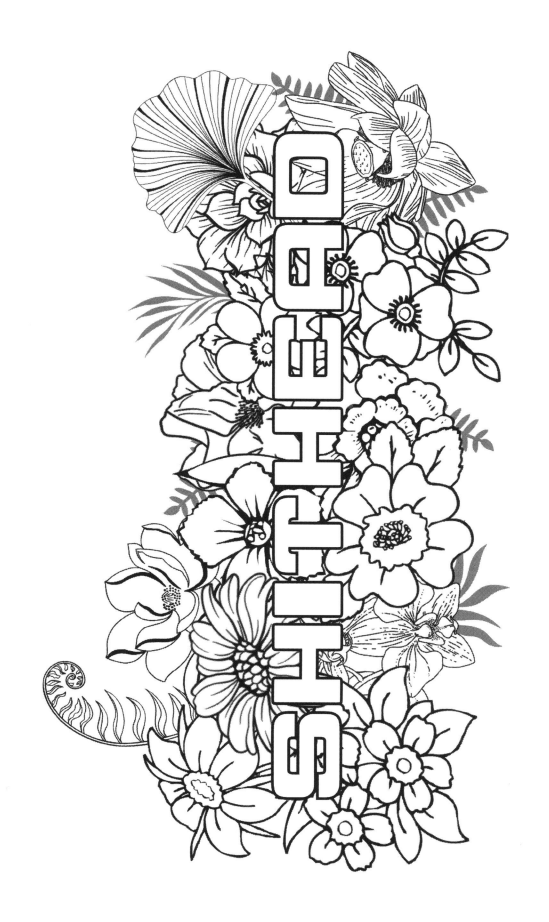

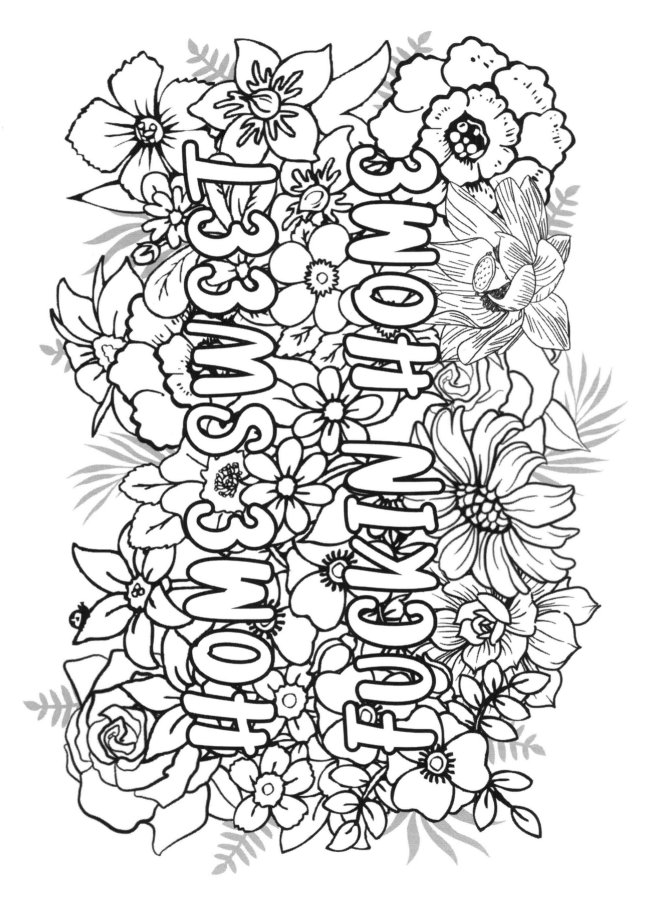

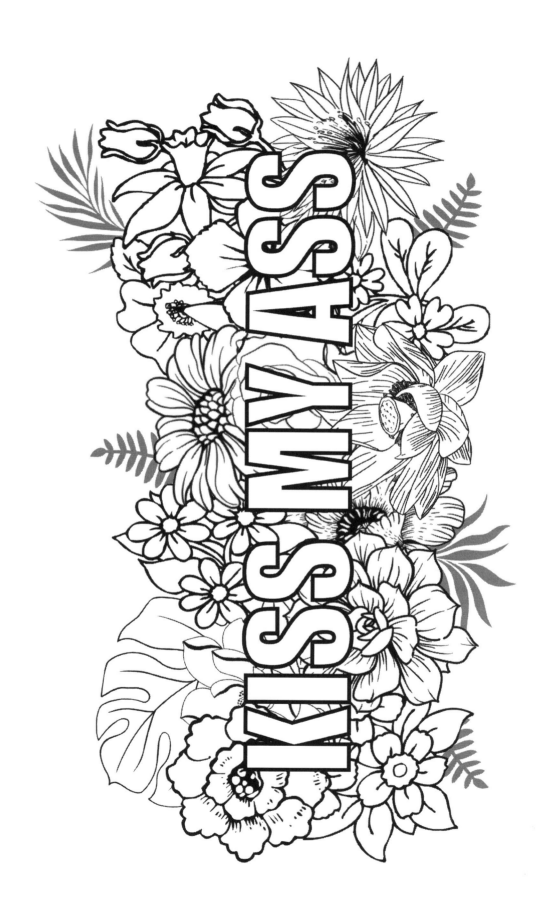

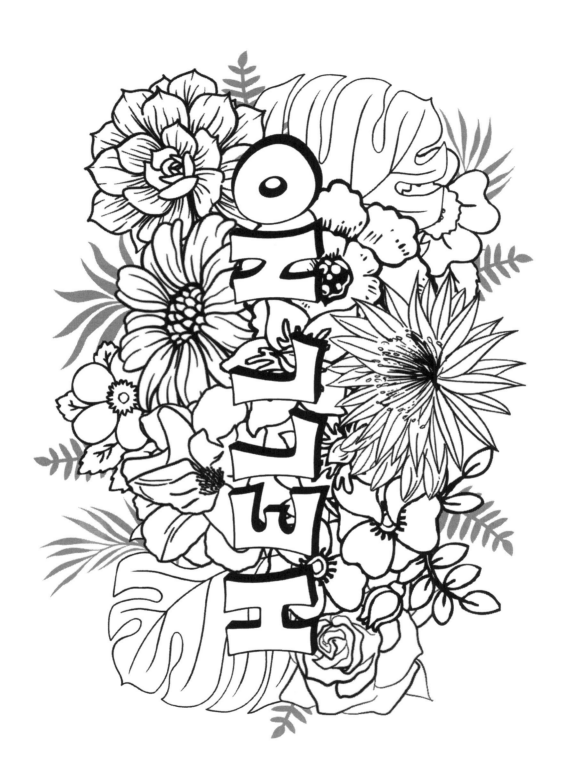

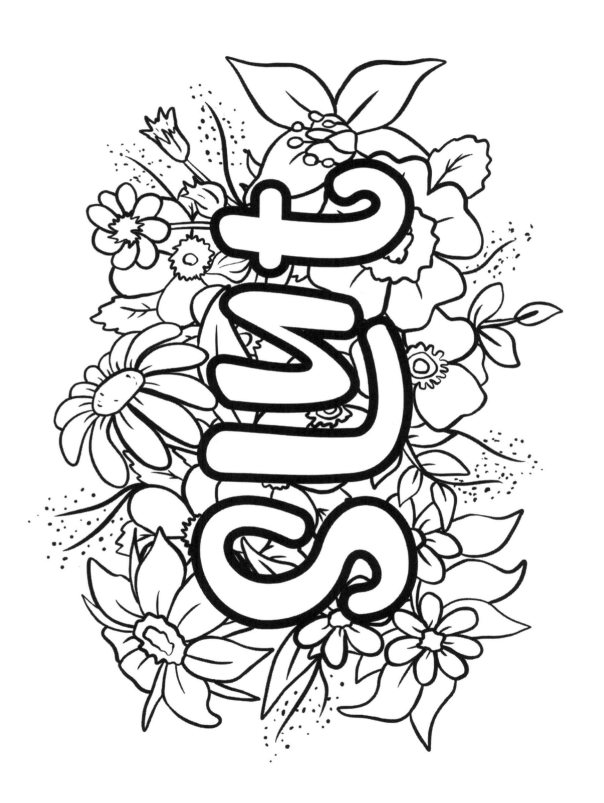

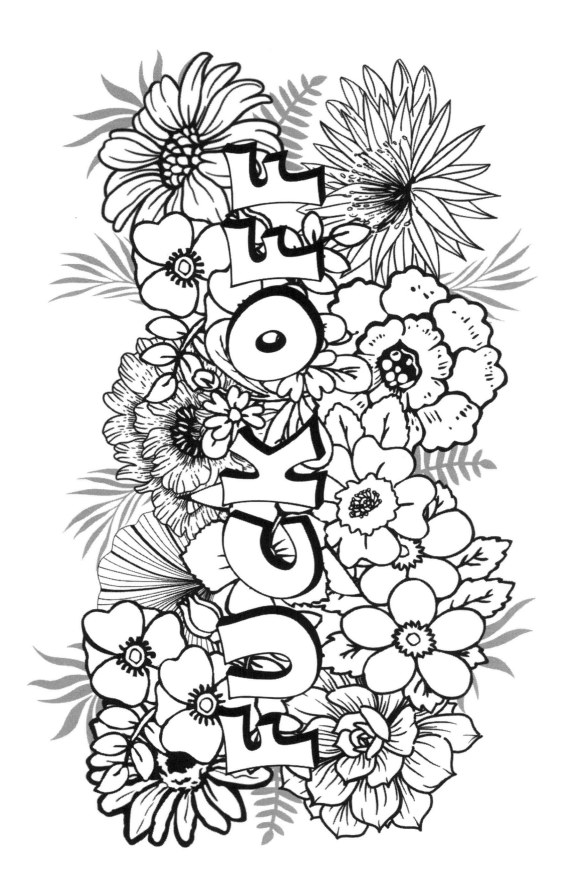

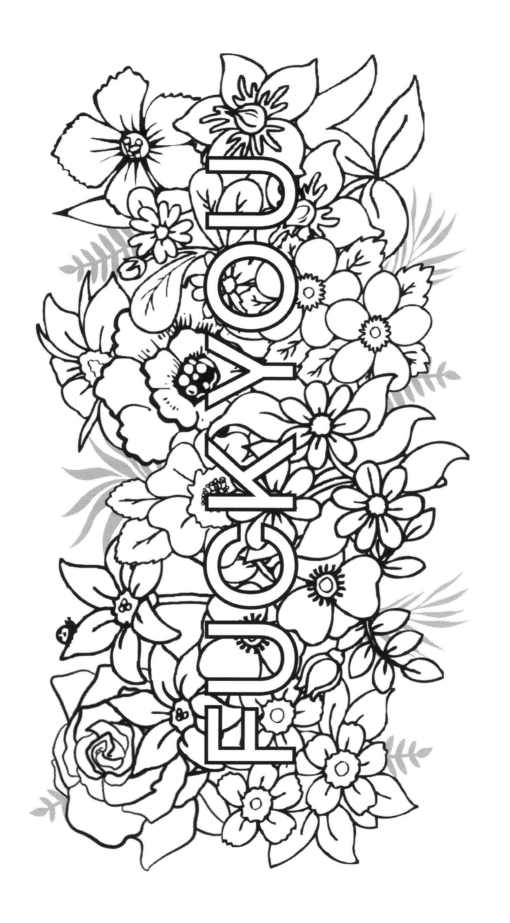

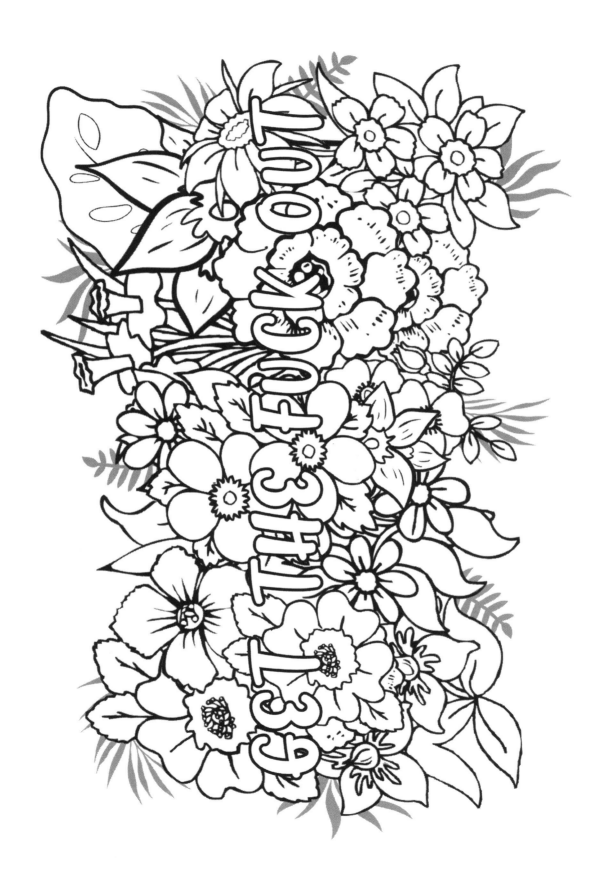

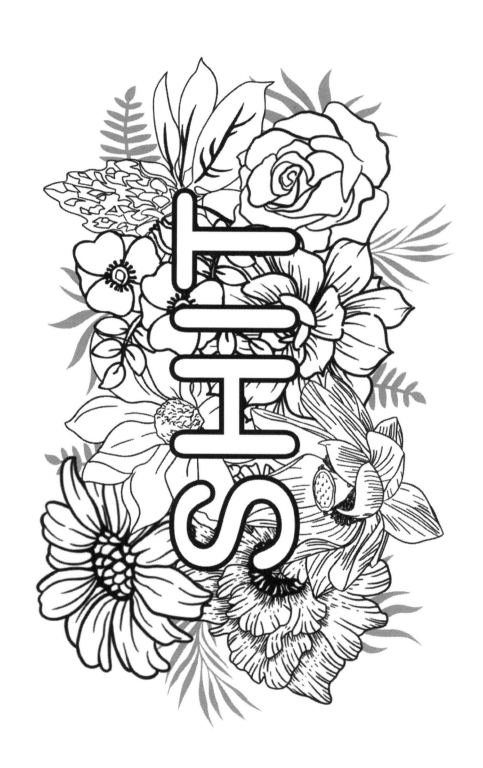

Made in the USA
Middletown, DE
29 October 2023

41501601R00038